MW01140071

DISCARD

ALTERNATOR BOOKS™

PINK

POP POWERHOUSE

HEATHER E. SCHWARTZ

Lerner Publications ◆ Minneapolis

Lerner Publications Company
An imprint of Lerner Publishing Group, Inc.
241 First Avenue North
Minneapolis, MN 55401 USA

For reading levels and more information, look up this title at www.lernerbooks.com.

Main body text set in Aptifer Sans LT Pro.
Typeface provided by Linotype AG.

Editor: Brianna Kaiser

Library of Congress Cataloging-in-Publication Data

Names: Schwartz, Heather E., author.
Title: P!nk : pop powerhouse / Heather E. Schwartz.
Other titles: Pink
Description: Minneapolis : Lerner, 2022. | Series: Boss lady bios (alternator books®) | Includes bibliographical references and index. | Audience: Ages 8–12 | Audience: Grades 4–6 | Summary: "Pop powerhouse P!nk has taken the music world by storm, producing hit singles and receiving numerous awards. This title tells about her journey to success and how she uses that success to help others" — Provided by publisher.
Identifiers: LCCN 2020026122 (print) | LCCN 2020026123 (ebook) | ISBN 9781728404530 (library binding) | ISBN 9781728417677 (ebook)
Subjects: LCSH: P!nk, 1979– —Juvenile literature. | Singers—United States—Biography—Juvenile literature.
Classification: LCC ML3930.P467 S3 2022 (print) | LCC ML3930.P467 (ebook) | DDC 782.42164092 [B]—dc23

LC record available at https://lccn.loc.gov/2020026122
LC ebook record available at https://lccn.loc.gov/2020026123

Manufactured in the United States of America
1-48511-49025-3/1/2021

TABLE OF CONTENTS

STRONG ROLE MODEL

P!NK STOOD IN FRONT OF A LARGE CROWD AT THE 2017 MTV VIDEO MUSIC AWARDS. She had just received the Video Vanguard Award for her impact and contribution to music. She began her acceptance speech with a story about her daughter to share an important message.

She described how her six-year-old daughter had recently called herself ugly. P!nk was horrified. She told her daughter

that people sometimes call her ugly too. But she wasn't changing and her daughter didn't need to either.

P!nk told the audience, "And I said to her, 'Do you see me growing my hair?' She said, 'No, mama.' I said, 'Do you see me changing my body?' 'No, mama.' 'Do you see me changing the way I present myself to the world?' 'No, mama.' 'Do you see me selling out arenas all over the world?' 'Yes, mama.'"

The audience erupted in cheers before P!nk continued. "We don't change," she said. "And we help other people to change so they can see more kinds of beauty."

P!nk ended her speech by thanking all the artists in the audience for being true to themselves and inspiring others. She had grown a lot since her start as a singer and performer, and she had become a role model to millions of fans.

P!nk and her daughter, Willow, pose at the 2017 MTV Video Music Awards.

CHAPTER 1
WILD CHILD

BEFORE P!NK WAS P!NK, SHE WAS ALECIA BETH MOORE. Alecia was born on September 8, 1979, in Doylestown, Pennsylvania. She has an older brother, Jason. Her parents are Jim Moore and Judith Moore.

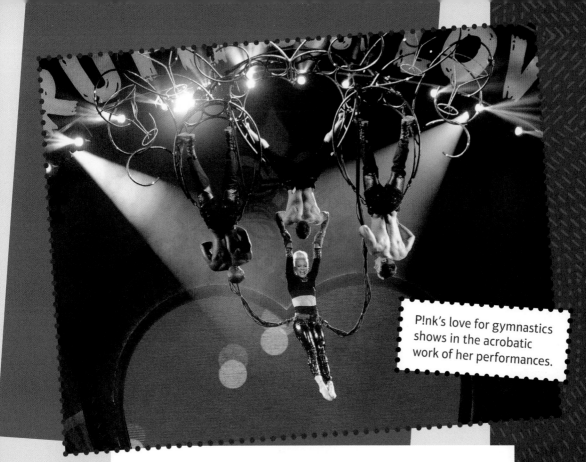

P!nk's love for gymnastics shows in the acrobatic work of her performances.

Alecia started gymnastics when she was four. She dreamed of going to the Olympics when she was older, but her coach dropped her from the team when she was twelve. Alecia was upset and was also hurting from her parents' divorce. She started to take advantage of her parents living apart. She would tell one parent she was at the other parent's house for the night. Instead, she'd go to clubs with her friends. "I was never allowed to go over to any of my friends' houses when I was little, because I was a bad influence," she later said. "None of their parents liked me and my own parents were scared to death of me—and for me."

When Alecia was a teenager, she sang at a club in Philadelphia every Friday night. The club wasn't the only place Alecia let her voice ring out. She also sang in a gospel choir, and she joined a punk band when she was fourteen. She started writing her own songs too. She went on to sing with the R&B groups Basic Instinct and Choice.

While Alecia was getting ahead in music, the rest of her life was out of control. She was partying and taking drugs. She even started selling drugs.

P!nk sang with multiple bands before starting her solo career.

P!nk once worked at fast-food restaurants, including McDonalds.

When Alecia was fifteen, she nearly overdosed. She decided to stop taking drugs, but the road to recovery wasn't without bumps. Alecia fought with her mother, got kicked out of her mother's house, and dropped out of high school.

She went to work at fast-food restaurants like Pizza Hut, McDonald's, and Wendy's, but those jobs didn't fuel her dreams. So she kept singing. She continued working with Choice and their record label, LaFace Records.

P!nk at the 2000 *Billboard* Music Awards

CHAPTER 2
ON HER OWN

IN 1998 P!NK BEGAN HER CAREER AS A SOLO ARTIST.
She earned her GED (an alternative to a high school diploma)
and continued working with LaFace Records. By then she'd
taken the name she'd use throughout her career: P!nk. She got

The members of *NSYNC, *left to right, back row,* Chris Kirkpatrick, Justin Timberlake, Lance Bass, *front row,* Joey Fatone, and JC Chasez in 1998

the name from a movie. P!nk got to work and released her first album, *Can't Take Me Home,* in April 2000. That month she signed on to tour as the opening act for the then popular boy band *NSYNC.

GETTING IT DONE!

Can't Take Me Home went double-platinum. Two of P!nk's singles from the album, "There You Go" and "Most Girls," made the *Billboard* Hot 100 Top 10 list.

P!nk was happy with her album. She liked writing songs that came from her own experiences. But soon she realized the songs on the album didn't really showcase the sound she wanted. She felt the album wasn't emotional or edgy enough. "There was no blood, sweat, or tears on my first album," she said. "And no emotional exchange between me and the musicians."

P!nk won the Female New Artist of the Year award at the 2000 *Billboard* Music Awards.

From left to right: P!nk, Mýa, Lil' Kim, and Christina Aguilera at the 2001 MTV Video Music Awards

In spring 2001, P!nk collaborated with Christina Aguilera, Mýa, and Lil' Kim to remake "Lady Marmalade" for the *Moulin Rouge!* soundtrack. Later that year, she also worked on her second album, *M!ssundaztood*. She pushed herself to be more authentic in both her lyrics and her sound.

GETTING IT DONE!

In 2002 the "Lady Marmalade" collaboration won a Grammy Award for Best Pop Collaboration with Vocals.

From left to right: P!nk, Christina Aguilera, and Mýa pose with their Grammy Awards in 2002.

P!nk's songs for *M!ssundaztood* showcased her own feelings she had about her family. The album helped open up communication with her parents and even led them to family therapy. She said the album was a conversation she started to have with herself.

"NOBODY HAD ANY IDEA WHO I REALLY WAS. NEITHER DID I—I WAS STILL TRYING TO FIGURE IT OUT."

P!nk's efforts to get in touch with her inner self seemed to be working. When *M!ssundaztood* came out in November, critics admired her for taking chances and being more personal. More than ten million copies of the album were sold worldwide.

P!nk's second album, *M!ssundaztood*, was an international hit.

P!nk with her father, Jim Moore, in 2000

CHAPTER 3
ROCK STAR LIFE

M!SSUNDAZTOOD **HELPED P!NK FIND HERSELF AND HER SOUND.** But promoting the album wore her out. Every interview felt like a therapy session because she was always talking about her parents' divorce.

"I WAS SO BURNT OUT BY THE END OF THAT CYCLE THAT I DIDN'T CARE. I DIDN'T WANT TO TALK ABOUT ANYTHING PERSONAL. I DIDN'T WANT TO WRITE ABOUT ANYTHING DEEP. I JUST WANTED TO MAKE A FUN . . . RECORD."

So P!nk decided to turn her attention to making a fun recording. She wrote new songs with producer and cowriter Tim Armstrong, a member of the punk band Rancid. When her third album, *Try This*, was released in 2003, her single "Trouble" stood out. It won P!nk a Grammy for Best Female Rock Vocal Performance in 2004. "Trouble" was her first solo Grammy.

P!nk and Carey Hart in 2006

By the age of twenty-five, P!nk was juggling fame and a career. She also had a relationship with motocross star Carey Hart. They had dated and broken up in the past, but P!nk knew they had something special. In the summer of 2005, she went to one of Hart's motocross races in Mammoth Lakes, California. At the race, she held up a sign asking him to marry her. He stopped racing and accepted her proposal.

The couple married in Costa Rica in January 2006. And P!nk's career kept moving full-steam ahead. She released her fourth album, *I'm Not Dead,* in April 2006, and soon left on a worldwide tour.

P!nk and Hart both had busy schedules. Over time, they struggled to make their relationship work, and they broke up after two years of marriage. P!nk put all of her feelings into songs for her fifth album, *Funhouse.*

P!nk performs in Manchester, England, on her Funhouse tour in 2009.

P!nk traveled to North America, Europe, and Australia for her Funhouse tour.

" 'Funhouse' was my divorce record. Carey and I had split and I was on my own and just a little bit wild. I remember, I hadn't spoken to Carey for, like, eight months and it was really painful for me," she said. "And I made one of my best records from heartbreak."

YOU'RE THE BOSS

P!nk expresses painful feelings and experiences in her songs. Writing about her problems helps her heal in a creative way.

Everyone has problems. You can deal with your problems in creative ways too. When you're angry, sad, or frustrated, express your feelings through art. You could write a story or poem about it. You could paint or draw a picture. You could even compose a song.

Then you might feel better. You will also have something positive—like a song or story—that you created from a negative situation.

P!nk and Carey Hart at the Grammy Awards in 2010

CHAPTER 4

MORE THAN MUSIC

FUNHOUSE **HELPED P!NK** tell Hart how she felt. She played him her song "I Don't Believe You" and wore her wedding dress in the music video. She also convinced Hart to appear with her in the music video for her song "So What." Soon the couple was back together and in couples' therapy.

P!nk sings on her The Truth about Love tour in 2013.

In June 2011, P!nk and Hart had their first child, Willow Sage. P!nk was a working mom and put out her sixth album, *The Truth about Love*, in 2012. Her family went on tour with her in 2013, and she earned close to $148 million in ticket sales.

GETTING IT DONE!

P!nk won her third Grammy for her collaboration on a remake of the song "Imagine" in 2011.

With her career in high gear, P!nk explored more ways to use her talents. She wrote songs for other singers, including Cher and Celine Dion. She acted in the movie *Thanks for Sharing.* She also started working with UNICEF, a charity that helps children around the world. And she posed in an ad for PETA, a group that works for animal rights.

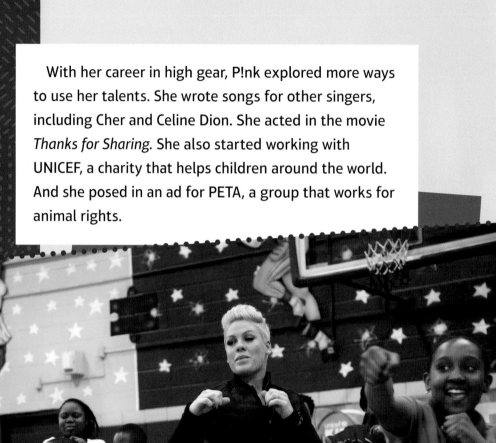

P!nk exercises with children at a UNICEF Kid Power event in 2015.

P!nk and Hart had their second child, Jameson Moon, in 2016. The following year, she released her seventh album, *Beautiful Trauma.* It was hard for P!nk to keep working as much as she did, but she felt singing was an important part of who she was as a person and a parent.

"I WANT TO BE THE BEST MOM IN THE WORLD. . . . AND I WANT TO FOLLOW MY PASSION TOO. I WANT MY KIDS TO SEE WHAT IT LOOKS LIKE TO HAVE A MOM THAT'S A BOSS."

P!nk is surrounded by her family at her star on the Hollywood Walk of Fame in 2019.

In 2018 P!nk sang at the Grammys and performed the national anthem at the Super Bowl. In 2019 she released her eighth album, *Hurts 2B Human*. That year she was honored with a star on the Hollywood Walk of Fame.

At the end of 2019, P!nk announced she was taking a break from music so she could focus on her family. Then, in early 2020, the worldwide COVID-19 pandemic reached the US. P!nk and three-year-old Jameson were

diagnosed with COVID-19 in March. She was terrified to see him so sick. Hart and Willow did not get sick, and P!nk and Jameson slowly recovered. When P!nk was well again, she donated $1 million to coronavirus relief.

While much of the world was in quarantine due to the pandemic, P!nk chose to focus on the positive and enjoy time with her family. She continues to stay dedicated to her true self. Fans can't wait to see what this self-assured superstar and activist does next!

P!nk and her son, Jameson Moon, in 2018

TIMELINE

1979   Alecia Beth Moore is born on September 8 in Doylestown, Pennsylvania.

2000   P!nk releases her first album, *Can't Take Me Home*.

2004   P!nk wins a Grammy for Best Female Vocal Performance for her song "Trouble."

2006   P!nk marries motocross star Carey Hart and releases her fourth album, *I'm Not Dead*.

2012   P!nk releases her sixth album, *The Truth about Love*.

2017   P!nk wins the Video Vanguard Award for her contribution to music.

2019   P!nk releases her eighth album, *Hurts 2B Human*.

2020   P!nk recovers from COVID-19 and takes a break from music to be with her family.

GLOSSARY

album: a collection of recordings such as those on a record or CD

authentic: real or genuine

lyrics: the words in a song

overdose: taking a very dangerous amount of a drug

pandemic: when a disease spreads very quickly and affects a large number of people over a wide area or throughout the world

producer: someone in charge of making and sometimes providing money for an album

punk: a type of rock music

quarantine: when people stay away from others to prevent a disease from spreading

R&B: a type of music that combines rhythm, blues, and pop

therapy: treatment to help someone feel better and grow stronger

SOURCE NOTES

5   Julia Zorthian, " 'We Don't Change.' Read Pink's Emotional VMA's Speech about Body Image and Her Daughter," *Time*, August 28, 2017, https://time.com /4918579/pink-vma-speech-daughter-transcript/.

5   Zorthian.

7   "Pink Biography," Biography, April 7, 2020, https:// www.biography.com/musician/pink.

12   "Pink Biography."

14   James Patrick Herman, "A Pink Retrospective: The Singer Dives into Her Seven Studio Albums," *Variety*, February 5, 2019, https://variety.com/2019/music /news/pink-albums-discography-interview -1203128555/.

17   Herman.

20   Herman.

25   "Pink on Life, Kids and Husband Carey Hart," YouTube video, 21:20, posted by *Entertainment Tonight*, April 18, 2018, https://www.youtube.com /watch?v=Ej-Cj6UgmkA.

LEARN MORE

Baxter, Roberta. *Women in Music*. Minneapolis: Abdo, 2019.

Grammy Awards: P!nk
https://www.grammy.com/grammys/artists/pnk/5201

Leigh, Anna. *Write and Record Your Own Songs*. Minneapolis: Lerner Publications, 2018.

P!nk
https://www.pinkspage.com/home/

Pink Biography
https://www.biography.com/musician/pink

RCA Records: P!nk
https://www.rcarecords.com/artist/pnk/

Schwartz, Heather E. *Ariana Grande: Music Superstar*. Minneapolis: Lerner Publications, 2021.

UNICEF
https://www.unicef.org

INDEX

PHOTO ACKNOWLEDGMENTS

Image credits: AP Photo/Matt Sayles, pp. 4, 18; AP Photo/Jordan Strauss/ Invision, p. 5; SevenMaps/Shutterstock.com, p. 6; yakub88/Shutterstock .com, p. 7; Christina Radish/Redferns/Getty Images, p. 8; ATIKAN PORNCHAIPRASIT/Shutterstock.com, p. 9; Ron Galella, Ltd./Ron Galella Collection/Getty Images, p. 10; Bevis AP Images/Nickel/SULUPRESS.DE, p. 11; Reuters/Alamy Stock Photo, p. 12; TIMOTHY A.CLARY/AFP/Getty Images, p. 13; Reuters/Alamy Stock Photo, p. 14; WRESPhotography/ Alamy Stock Photo, p. 15; AP Photo/Eric Jamison, p. 16; AP Photo/Jon Super, p. 19; AP Photo/MTI, Peter Kollanyi, p. 20; AP Photo/Chris Pizzello, p. 22; Gonzales Photo/Alamy Stock Photo, p. 23; AP Photo/Charles Sykes/ Invision, p. 24; AP Images/Sipa USA, p. 26; TNYF/WENN.com/Alamy Stock Photo p. 27.

Cover: Jeff Spicer/Getty Images.